SECOND CHANCES

JASON SIMMONS

authorHOUSE®

AuthorHouse™
1663 Liberty Drive
Bloomington, IN 47403
www.authorhouse.com
Phone: 1 (800) 839-8640

Although based on a true story, significant events have been changed for dramatic effect.

This is a work of fiction. All of the characters, names, incidents, organizations, and dialogue in this novel are either the products of the author's imagination or are used fictitiously.

Published by AuthorHouse 08/27/2019

ISBN: 978-1-7283-2457-9 (sc)
ISBN: 978-1-7283-2456-2 (e)

Print information available on the last page.

Any people depicted in stock imagery provided by Getty Images are models, and such images are being used for illustrative purposes only. Certain stock imagery © Getty Images.

This book is printed on acid-free paper.

Although based on a true story, significant events
have been changed for dramatic effect.

CONTENTS

Prologue.. ix

PART 1
THE VOYAGE

Chapter 1 1
Chapter 2 11
Chapter 3 17
Chapter 4 23
Chapter 5 29
Chapter 6 35

PART 2
THE RAFT

Chapter 1 43
Chapter 2 49
Chapter 3 55
Chapter 4 61
Chapter 5 67
Chapter 6 73

PART 3
THE RESCUE

Chapter 1 79
Chapter 2 83

Epilogue.. 89
About The Author... 91

PROLOGUE

It was not your typical August morning in Los Angeles. The heat and humidity had already taken its toll on those who dared to venture outside. I was grateful for the air-conditioned corner office that offered a view of the bustling street below and watched with half-interest as people mopped their brows and hung their shoulders in defeat. As a fairly new reporter for the *Times* I was expected to earn my coveted office so rather than stare out the glistening window I set out to discover the perfect story for the editor. Turning from the window I focused on my desk, reached out and picked up the stack of letters that had accumulated in a far corner. Quickly thumbing through what looked like the usual junk mail I finally came to rest on a small envelope with a Miami postmark. Tearing it open I recognized immediately the stationary with the anchor logo. Deja vu, I thought to myself, for I had received a similar invitation nearly two years ago. It too had been for a Bon Voyage party, and although that particular one had sounded intriguing, I didn't go. Miami was clear across the country, and if the humidity was bad here it would have been a killer there and quite honestly the last thing I wanted to do was to attend a party for two people who were attempting to sail around the world in what I considered to be a very small boat on a very big ocean. Pure madness! Besides, the rumors were that they weren't even getting along. Lorenzo had been living up to his reputation as a real latin lover and Karen had been taking out her wrath on everybody and everything. She'd been having dreams, bad dreams … she called them omens. And if anyone believed in omens, it was Karen. She had put up with a lot over the years, and she had always relied on her dreams to guide her. It was her second sight, we all joked. Oddly enough, she was usually right.

Now a second invitation and if my suspicions were correct, a real opportunity to deliver the very story my editor sought, but I'm getting ahead of myself, so let me take you back to the beginning, a story that began nearly two years ago in Florida.

PART 1

THE VOYAGE

CHAPTER 1

The *Mysteria* wallowed in the trough then shuddered helplessly as the walls of water crashed over her deck. Great tridents of lightning pierced the darkness, chased by nearly deafening bursts of thunder. The angry voices coming from the small cabin below rose to a pitch then like the storm outside, sputtered into silence. It was only a few minutes before the man appeared on deck and as the small sailboat lurched to one side he rolled the lifeless body over the rail.

Her throat tightened, convulsed, then sucked in the precious air as Karen bolted upright in her bed. The silk night dress she wore clung to her wet body, defining her ample figure. Her hands shook as she reached across the night stand for the familiar glass of water. The nightmares were becoming all too frequent. But what frightened her most was that they were always the same, so real that she could feel herself slipping away, the black sea pulling her down and filling her lungs. Too real, Karen thought, to be anything less than a warning. She believed in omens and this one was telling her that she had no business attempting to sail around the world. Looking back, she could vaguely remember the time when shortly after they had met and fallen in love she and Lorenzo had talked about such adventures, sailing the seven seas, island hopping and blending with the locals, but that was years ago and in spite of the fact that they were both equally capable sailors the reality was that life had gotten in the way. Lorenzo's broken promises had revealed that her once loving husband had returned to his philandering ways, his indiscretions were no longer indiscreet, leaving her embarrassed, ashamed and in a marriage that was filled with constant bickering. Her heart had been broken far too many times and even if it had been her husband's lifelong dream to sail the world, it just was not hers now. Karen was not about to leave the rest of her family, board a sloop, and sail off with the very man she was ready to divorce! He could take anyone, there were several seamen as capable as herself, so why make her feel guilty for not wanting to go? The dark thoughts crept back into her mind ... was he really capable of murder? Could he be so cold that he could just toss her overboard in the middle of the Pacific? She believed he could, and it always came back to the dream, Karen's dream that is.

Excited voices drifted up through the open bedroom window that overlooked the sloping back lawn where party tables had been decorated in a nautical theme. Colored lanterns had been strung across the yard and down along the dock where the *Mysteria* was moored. Karen stood and peered below. Lorenzo was chatting up the ladies as usual.

"He'll never change," she whispered to herself. How many times had she asked for a divorce? Too many. His answer was always the same,

"The church won't allow it, you know that, so let's just try to work this out." Then would come the rehearsed promises that echoed in Karen's head, promises that she had heard so many times she could recite them. Useless, hollow, empty words simply meant to pacify her, but she knew he was as fed up as she was and had even told her as much, yet in spite of the years of marriage he was unwilling to part with so much as a single dollar. He would just continue to do as he pleased. True, Lorenzo had loved her once, but she now sensed a deep hatred seething beneath his suave exterior. She wondered if his first wife had sensed the very same thing before taking her life. Lorenzo had long ago explained Lydia's death, but now Karen had more questions than answers.

The shouts from below stirred Karen from her reverie, then she brushed her fingers gently across the small gold locket that had hung from her neck since childhood, a reminder of the generations of women that had worn it before her ... they were strong, independent and survivors. "You won't be rid of me so easily, Lorenzo," she snarled.

Karen looked beyond her husband and could see Lorenzo's sons lifting the old steel tub into the dingy. Loading it to the brim with ice they quickly transferred case after case of beer, soda, and nearly every other beverage imaginable. They had positioned it on the dock next to the gangplank so that the guests would feel free to select something before boarding. The

Mysteria glistened in the morning sun. She had been dressed from stem to stern and even Karen had to admit that she looked inviting. She was a handsome boat, old but quite seaworthy and Karen and Lorenzo had spent the better part of twenty years sailing her along the Eastern coast. Karen focused on the colored flags that draped from the mast of the sailboat; she knew she wasn't ready to sail across the Pacific any more than she was ready for this damn party. Dozens of invitations had been sent, friends from all over the country were arriving for what promised to be the Bon Voyage party of the year. So little time, Karen thought to herself, but to tell Lorenzo today that she would not be sailing with him wasn't quite right. Let him have his silly party and strut for the women, as she knew he would. His reputation as a womanizer was well known and caused endless problems in their marriage. Let him have his day, she mused, she would have hers soon enough. He wasn't scheduled to sail for at least another week, she'd tell him tomorrow and in the meantime she needed to brace herself for the stream of people that seemingly wished her well.

"Josh," Lorenzo hailed his stepson from the end of the short pier, "see what's keeping your mother, would you? She should have been down here nearly an hour ago." The edge in his voice betrayed his irritation. He chastised himself silently, he could see the puzzled look on Josh's face and the last thing he needed now was for Karen's son to question his intent. He had planned her demise so carefully. He had to convince not only Karen but her son as well that she should sail with him. He had to be rid of his wife once and for all. He couldn't bear another argument, another plea for divorce or alimony. He just figured that it was a very big ocean and there would be plenty of time to create the perfect tragedy. He didn't expect though to be met with such fierce resistance. Lorenzo never believed for a moment that his wife wouldn't make the voyage. But right now he didn't have time for her theatrics; he was tired of hearing about her premonitions and he was even more tired of her endless excuses. In all reality he was tired of her. She had used nearly every argument imaginable, that her mother was getting on in years, yet Karen's children were grown and perfectly capable of looking after their grandmother. Then she insisted that she couldn't be out of touch with her family. He had carefully explained to Karen that she could catch a plane back from almost any port at any given time. They had a sophisticated radio system on board and would be in constant communication with her children. If an emergency arose Lorenzo felt sure they would be contacted. His own children had assured them both that they would look after things in their father's absence, including Karen's overanxious brood.

Looking across the lawn Lorenzo could see his wife making her way toward the dock from the house. It took only a moment for him to remember the day he had met Karen. She was standing on the pier drink in hand as he pulled up to the dock. He recognized the small group of friends that crowded around her, mesmerized by her beauty. He had met and bedded a lot of ladies but never had he seen anyone as striking as this woman. She captured his heart, he remembered, as she threw her head back in genuine laughter, her wispy, blond hair brushing across her face in the light sea breeze. It was at that instant that he was determined to have her and have her he did. She had known exactly the kind of man he was when they first met, friends had warned her of his playboy ways and even he had told her to expect nothing less. The courtship was brief, the passion intense, and after only a few short months they married. In spite of the years Lorenzo believed Karen was just as beautiful today as the day he married her but time had been unkind in so many other ways. She had become nothing less than a shrew, constantly complaining, endlessly nagging, and even her attempts to change him had only fallen on deaf ears. He wondered now why he had ever remarried. Once should have been enough, but Karen was not only beautiful, she was persuasive and had caught him at a weak moment. Now he watched silently as she walked onto the patio and was quickly swallowed up by the dozens of people who had come to see them off. It irritated him that she stopped to chat with first one couple then another as if she was deliberately putting off the inevitable meeting with him rather than welcome their guests together.

"Savannah, Bill, how wonderful to see you both," she blurted, "and you came all the way from Georgia for this?"

Savannah drawled, "Why on Earth would we miss it? The adventure of a lifetime is about to begin." Pulling her hostess off to one side she said, "Come, let's chat. Things must be perking up between you two, I mean, sailing around the world? I'm a firm believer in kiss and make up but this? And what about all those dreams you've been having, not to mention Lorenzo's roaming eye! Something tells me that dog won't hunt!" Savannah had her charms and had always delighted Karen with her Southern way of expressing things.

"Savannah, you know very well that I don't intend to go, I just haven't told him yet. I'm scared to death. I know the dreams are warnings and this could all end so badly. I'm sure he'll be reasonable and take someone else if he insists on going, although I've discouraged him as much as I can."

"You know better than I do honey, that once Lorenzo has made up his mind he's not likely to change it. Listen Karen, you're wise to be afraid, and even if he is offering the proverbial olive branch, unfortunately tragedy seems to follow the man. We can all agree that it's a very small boat, need I say more?"

"Believe me, Savannah, you're not telling me anything I don't already know, and even if he really means this to be our reconciliation, I believe it's too little too late. I'm petrified ... not only of the trip but of him. There's just something about him that isn't quite right."

Savannah could see Karen's trembling hands and the fear in her eyes was obvious. "Girlfriend," Savannah said sternly, "Lorenzo has had his share of problems, true, but surely he wouldn't deliberately hurt you?"

Karen hesitated, "I wouldn't put it past him, I just don't trust him anymore, I keep thinking about poor Lydia."

"Karen, Lydia wasn't well, we all knew that they were both miserable. She took the only way out she knew."

"Did she really?" Before Savannah could react Karen gave a quick hug to her old friend. She didn't want to think about Lydia anymore, she knew she had to calm herself before turning toward the pier where Lorenzo was waiting. He seemed impatient, pacing back and forth like some kind of caged tiger.

"About time you decided to grace us with your presence," he snapped as she made her way toward him. In an effort to soften his harsh greeting Lorenzo took her elbow and guided her toward the *Mysteria*. "Take a look at your new home my dear," he coaxed, "she's all spruced up for the occasion and ready for an inspection from the first mate!"

Reaching the gangplank, Karen hesitated, then pushed forward. Cautiously, she examined the sailboat hoping to find some problem, she prayed there'd be an obvious oversight that could postpone the sailing date.

"Look Karen, as you asked, I've plotted a course that will take us to the Bahamas. I realize that you have friends in Nassau that you'd like to see, in spite of that fact that it's out of the way and it will take a good deal longer to get to the Canal."

"Well, pardon me, skipper, but I didn't know we were on a deadline. This wasn't meant to be some kind of race ... it was supposed to be a pleasure trip. Do you even know what a pleasure trip is?"

Slamming his beer on the table he replied sarcastically, "Yes, my dear, I *know* what a pleasure trip is. I was just trying to avoid any bad weather by getting to Panama a bit sooner. You know how you hate sailing in bad weather, but if it'll make you happy we'll go by way of Nassau."

Turning her back to him she continued her review. After her inspection she reluctantly agreed that the *Mysteria* was ready.

"And the radio? Is it finally working?"

"Just a little tweaking and it'll be good as they get," he assured her.

"Well, you've seen to everything, skipper, right down to the last detail. I hate to admit it," she said convincingly, "but she's ready to sail, so let's just enjoy the party and discuss the details later."

"What's there to discuss?" Lorenzo shot back. "We've waited a lifetime for this trip; no more excuses, no more delays, we'll just go. You and me."

"Fine. Whatever. Now I'm going topside to be sociable, coming?"

Karen couldn't wait to escape the confines of the small cabin and nearly flew down the ramp to the dock. She mingled with the throng of people attending and tried to keep as much distance from Lorenzo as she could, knowing that he wouldn't hesitate to brace her about the trip even in front of all their friends. The party was a huge success, lasting till the late hours and capped off with a dazzling fireworks display. As the last of the revelers made their way out the gate Josh guided his mother to the house and took her aside.

"Well, did you tell the good captain?"

"No. I'll tell him first thing in the morning. You know Lorenzo's temper, I didn't want a scene."

"Mother, you simply have to tell him. You couldn't possibly be of any use to him as frightened as you are. He'll understand. It doesn't really matter what the reason, if you don't *feel* safe you won't *be* safe. It's just too risky."

"Please, Josh, let me handle this my way," Karen whispered as she rushed her son out the door. "I'll call you first thing, promise."

She turned to go upstairs and saw Lorenzo standing on the landing outside the bedroom. As he glared down at her Karen felt a small prickle at the nape of her neck. She had to be firm.

"How can you do this?" he demanded. "Are you going to force me to make this trip alone? This was supposed to be *our* dream. Sail the seven seas, you said, forget the rest of the world, you said. And now?"

"I simply told you what you wanted to hear, Lorenzo. That was then, when it was just a dream. This is now and you think it should be a reality. Well, the reality is that I don't want to go. The timing is bad for one thing. My mother's not well and needs me. You and I are at each other's throats most of the time. Why on earth can't you just ask someone else to crew? Have your damn dream ... just have it without me! I'm not going and that's final. End of discussion."

Karen pushed by him on her way to the bedroom. She slid through the door quickly and locked it behind her. She was in no mood to put up with him this evening. Let him sleep off the booze and perhaps tomorrow she could reason with him, or even better, he'll just accept her decision.

Lorenzo winced as he heard the bolt slide on the bedroom door. He knew her mind was made up. He'd been fighting it for weeks but now she was adamant, there would be no budging her. He was fed up with the argument, fed up with her. Hell, I'll just play it by ear he thought to himself. Ramon, a longtime sailing buddy, could make the first leg to Nassau and who knows, maybe by then Karen would have a change of heart. She could be a bitch, he knew, but there was the occasional time when she could be a hell of a lot of fun and undoubtedly, she was the sexiest first mate on the Florida coast. The thought of Karen unexpectedly aroused him. Damn her for locking the door. He was angry and had had too much to drink, his head was swimming and he knew he had to curb his temper. Curling his large frame on the small twin bed of the guest quarters, Lorenzo tried to focus on the ceiling. Before the room could stop spinning he passed out.

CHAPTER 2

T he morning the *Mysteria* set sail Karen welcomed relief like an old friend. Lorenzo had finally agreed to take Ramon on the voyage and in spite of his anger he begrudgingly told Karen that he understood. She slept sounder that first night than she had in months. But by the third evening the dreams were again haunting her, only now Karen was not the victim. The storm raged as always but now it was the *Mysteria* that perished in the deep sea. The boat was in pieces, strewn across the base of a solitary crag that jutted up from the depths of the ocean. In spite of the heavy rain Karen could clearly see the splintered mast and debris of death that littered the water, yet never any sign of her husband. She'd wake in tears, calling for Lorenzo. When after seven days she finally heard from him, she was furious.

"What the hell is a radio for if you aren't going to use it?" she demanded. "You were supposed to call every third day without fail. Are you just getting even with me for not making the trip?"

"Take it easy, my dear. We arrived in Nassau safely. I guess the radio needed a little more than tweaking," he joked. "It's been on the fritz but I'm taking care of it. Right now I've got bigger problems. Ramon can't continue," he lied, "he slipped, broke his ankle, and is now sporting a somewhat restrictive, although very stylish cast." Lorenzo had tried to make light of the accident but then turned serious. "I need your help, Karen. I simply cannot do this alone. Please, *please* Karen, get on the next plane, meet me and at least sail to Hawaii with me. I promise you'll love it. It will be the most delightful adventure, one to tell the grandchildren!"

"Whose? Yours or mine? I knew you'd prey on my guilt, Lorenzo, but I'm still not convinced. The dreams are back, and I'm telling you that something terrible is going to happen, I just know it and I'm scared to death."

"Karen, they are only dreams. We couldn't be any safer if we were in your mother's arms. How about this," he bargained, "it's a short trip, ten days or so to the Canal, and I swear if I haven't convinced you that we were meant to take this trip I'll find a crew in Panama that will get me to Hawaii, fair enough?" Lorenzo believed that he had just offered the perfect compromise to her and her hesitation on the other end of the line told him that he was on the right track.

Karen was indeed having second thoughts. Her resolve was melting away, mainly because she was no longer the victim in her dreams ... he was. She had planned to use his absence to file for a divorce, she just wanted him out of her life, not dead. Were her dreams really an omen of what was to come she wondered or were they just the product of an overactive imagination? Was Ramon's injury yet another omen? Karen knew he could make it alone, although risky ... but if she agreed to go with Lorenzo how long would she be safe? How bad *was* their marriage? Karen was wavering now and she realized that he was leaving her with little choice, he was definitely playing the guilt card. She then reasoned that the sail to Panama wouldn't take long and they could join other boats heading the same direction.

"You promise I'll have a good time. You swear you won't make this miserable for both of us?"

Sensing her initial reluctance, Lorenzo had done his best to sound genuine. He knew he had to get her on the boat at any cost. There would be plenty of yachts making the short hop to Panama and he could visualize her socializing and settling in, all the while convincing her that his intentions to save their marriage were sincere. Getting her to Panama City was one thing, but continuing on to Hawaii was another. Somehow he had to keep her on that boat and once through the Canal and on the open sea he could accomplish whatever he wished.

"I promise. I swear. You have my solemn word, *mi amor*."

"Cut the crap. I'll be there tomorrow." Her hands shook as she hung up the phone, she felt guilty, angry and just plain scared. The next morning she managed to pack a bag, book a flight and make her way to the airport despite the concerned protests of her son. After voicing his opinion it seemed as though he had even less faith in Lorenzo than she did. Karen promised to call at the earliest opportunity and keep him advised of not only the trip but her husband's state of mind.

CHAPTER 3

The Caribbean sun was warm on Karen's back. Lorenzo, true to his word, had been most attentive and almost charming. But what was supposed to be a ten day sail to the Panama Canal was now entering its third week. The *Mysteria* had been sorely overloaded. That coupled with a windless sea had cut the motor-sailer to a snail's pace. Low on fuel, they had attempted to replenish the tanks at Great Inagua but tired in the long line of boats waiting at the refueling dock and decided to press on hoping for a stiff breeze. Now they regretted their haste, out of fuel and in a dead calm, they were at the mercy of Mother Nature. The other boats had left them behind as the *Mysteria* inched her way toward Panama. A small glass of wine in the evenings fortified Karen, but her good temperament was growing short and she deeply regretted ever having consented to the trip.

"Can't you please try that damn radio again," Karen pleaded. "It's been days and I'm sure Josh is worried sick."

"How many times can I say this Karen, we need parts that I just don't have onboard. I'll get them in the city and all will be fixed."

He had become such an accomplished liar that he knew she wouldn't question him and he had worried that with the trip taking longer than expected she would definitely want to talk to her son. Surely she would ask about Ramon, then she would find out he had not broken his ankle and then the great war would be on before they ever reached Panama City. He simply couldn't take a chance that she might learn of his lies. Lorenzo knew he had to keep her isolated from the mainland so early on he had disconnected the antenna from the back of the radio rendering it useless, a small procedure and one she would never notice. Still she begged him daily to turn it on. They had been out of contact with her son and daughter for three weeks. This was definitely not the experience she had been promised. By the time they reached the entrance to the canal Karen had managed to work herself into a frenzy.

"As soon as you get back from the Port Authority I'm catching the first flight home," she vowed. "I've had enough, I certainly didn't bargain for this and not having a radio was definitely not part of the deal," she raged.

The skipper had already gathered their passports and other valuables back in Nassau and hidden them in a safe place. By law only he, as captain of the boat, would be allowed to disembark, present identification of all crew and clear customs.

"We're good to go," Lorenzo smiled when after a few hours he stepped back onboard the *Mysteria* from the water taxi, and with a hint of sarcasm he added, "We've been legally accepted into Panama."

"Hold the shuttle," Karen screamed. "Get me off this boat! Get me off this damn boat right now."

"Mi Amor, calm yourself, the shuttle's waiting, go join your friends at the Yacht club, have a drink. Enjoy."

"Don't you *mi amor* me, you ... you ... you Latin louse! You will not sweet talk me into staying here another minute. Finished, you hear? I am absolutely finished with this and the first phone booth I come to I'm calling the children to tell them so!"

"Karen, you know you don't mean that. You're just upset that it took longer than we thought to get here. But now we've arrived, land ho and all that. Let's relax and have a good time. You know the moment you see your friends you'll be glad you came."

"Never!" She screamed back as she boarded the small launch which took her to shore. She cursed the sea legs that caused her to weave a path down the long pier until she stood at the entrance of a small hotel along the sea front. Directed to a telephone, Karen quickly dialed the number in Miami. "Josh," she wailed when her son's familiar voice answered the phone. "It's absolutely dreadful. I miss you and your sister terribly, and your grandmother, how is she? I have so many questions. The radio's been out for weeks and I've felt so isolated!"

"Mother, calm down, first, everyone is fine, including grandmother. We miss you as well. We figured you were having radio trouble. Ramon called as soon as he got back from Nassau and told us Lorenzo was fighting a losing battle with the damn thing. We knew you'd call the first chance you got."

"And how is the poor man? Rotten luck to break his ankle that way, but I heard he has quite a stylish cast!" Karen smiled at the sound of Josh's voice. Her children were everything to her. That she was overprotective would have been an understatement, but she was also overbearing, and that sometimes left her grown children feeling stifled. She detected a sense of independence in her son's tone and wondered if his newly found freedom hadn't influenced him. The slightest trace of jealousy crept over Karen as she listened to Josh explain how very well they were all getting on. Suddenly Josh stopped in mid sentence.

"Listen mother," he said anxiously. "Where did you get the idea that Ramon had broken his ankle? Yes, we spoke to him as soon as he got back, but we didn't see him until a few days ago ... and he didn't have any kind of cast on his leg. Did Lorenzo tell you Ramon had fallen? Why would he lie about that unless he had no other way to convince you to join him on the *Mysteria*? It just doesn't sound right to me mom, I think you need to come home as soon as possible."

Karen's face went pale, then flushed with anger. He lied, she thought to herself, about Ramon and what else? The radio? It probably worked just fine, he just didn't want me talking to the kids, knowing I would ask about the injury. And how would he explain that? She could barely wait to confront her husband, and was even more anxious to see how he would wiggle out of the latest lie.

"Josh, believe me, I've made it this far and I intend to stay just long enough to see a few friends, have a few drinks and catch a flight home. We'll talk again tomorrow after I've had a chance to discuss all of this with Lorenzo. I want you to call Ramon right now and find out about this ankle business. Look, I've gotta go for now so take care and don't worry, I'll be fine. Love you, now say goodbye."

Hearing the worry in her son's voice Karen hated to disconnect the telephone but she knew that it was time to face the truth. A confrontation was coming.

CHAPTER 4

The Panama Canal Yacht Club in Cristobal was an inviting oasis for those making the transition through the locks. Sailing from Nassau, Karen had first looked forward to this refreshing stop, now she couldn't wait to leave. Lorenzo had deliberately lied to her and she wanted to know why. She spotted her husband marching up the pier from the launch, he'd had enough time to secure the *Mysteria* and was now making his way toward her.

"Liar," she hissed as he took her arm, "Ramon no more broke his ankle than I did. Did you really think I wouldn't find out? All it took was one phone call, are you really going to try to deny it?" Turning her to face him he looked into her eyes.

"No, mi amor, I'm not going to deny it, but you wouldn't have come any other way. I've tried to show you how very much I love you, I've tried to be patient, but I have no control over the weather and never thought for a moment that it would take three weeks to get here. I honestly believed you would forgive my small lie and understand that it was only meant to have you near me. I just wanted one more chance to show you that I'm willing to change, to be the husband you once married."

Still furious, she continued, "And I suppose you lied about the radio as well, it's just like you to keep me from my children. I won't believe for a moment that it doesn't work perfectly."

"I swear to God Karen, the radio isn't working but I have every intention of getting right on that today. I can get the parts in town and if I have to work all night, so be it. I'm begging you to give me this last chance, stay, enjoy the Yacht Club, at least for a few days and it you haven't had a change of heart I'll find a new crew." He could almost believe it himself, these words he fabricated in an effort to keep her here.

Brushing the tears from her cheek Karen stared back at him.

"Very well, I'll do as you ask, but only because I want to take some time to get my head together, and it would probably do me good to be among friends. I'll call Josh tomorrow and let him know I'll be staying on a bit longer."

Karen's mind raced, she had done her best to keep her anger in check but she knew in her heart that he now had no intention of letting her leave Panama. She had learned over the years how to read him, she could see the deceit on his face and knew immediately that he was lying. In her haste to leave the *Mysteria* she had neglected to ask for her passport and credit cards, now she realized that he would never return them so the odds of her slipping out to the airport and getting on a plane back to Miami where she could file for divorce were slim and none. If I'm to survive this, she thought, I'll have to have a plan of my own.

For five days Karen and Lorenzo reveled in the company of fellow sailors. Like a ritual, they'd sit out on the veranda and swap sea stories, drink, dance and socialize late into the evenings, until the marina bells would signal the departure of the last launch for the moored boats. Once on board the *Mysteria*, Lorenzo would lure her to their bunk with nothing more than a scotch and a boyish grin. He would make love to her and end the evening holding Karen in his arms.

The slightest trace of a smile tugged at the corners of Karen's mouth.

"Why do I love you so? You're irresponsible, egocentric, and you chase anything in a skirt. Even tonight, mooning over those girls ... my God, they're young enough to be your daughters!"

"But they're not," he playfully retorted. "And I always come back to you, don't I?"

"You're not without your charm, I'll admit. But one of these days you'll go too far and you'll lose me forever. You really *are* a pig, you know?"

"Yes, but I'm *your* pig, mi amor." And for a brief moment he thought he might actually change his ways for her, then just as quickly he dismissed the notion as ridiculous. He was what his friends referred to as a man's man, a good old boy, the ultimate sailor. He was envied by many, denounced by some. He was simply who he was ... Lorenzo Orozco. He was feeling good, his plans were in motion. He had her right where he wanted her, on the *Mysteria* and ready to make the long haul across the Pacific.

"I wish I felt better about making this trip," Karen whispered. "I can't believe you've once again liquored me up and talked me into this. I still have half a mind to catch a plane home and leave you to it," she lied. She wasn't fooled by him, she'd already taken advantage of their stay at the Yacht Club to finalize her own plan, one where a divorce wasn't necessary. If Lorenzo wasn't going to let her leave the city she'd just have to beat him at his own game. She had already tried asking him for her things to no avail. He had simply refused, arguing that with the piracy rampant in the area their valuables were safer where he had hidden them. Going to the Consulate to replace her passport was out of the question too, she would have to prove that her life was in danger ... and she couldn't. Both the local police and the U.S. Embassy would just see it as a domestic dispute and not involve themselves. The Latino mentality worked against her as well, she was the lowly wife and her husband was king of the castle, the chauvinistic police would be no help to her. Karen believed she was left with only one recourse. She had managed to slip into town unnoticed and knowing that drugs were readily available for the right price, she discreetly purchased exactly what she needed. A small, white pill which she could place in her locket. She had been assured that it would kill instantly, no muss, no fuss. Karen had to be certain, though, that she could get to him before he got to her. Lorenzo had been rambling on while she was lost in thought, so she turned toward him as he continued.

"Look how much you've enjoyed the past few days," he cooed. "Karen, just imagine two more months of the same thing. The radio is working just fine now, so there's nothing to worry about. I really don't want to do this without you, you know that."

"Yes, but I don't know why. Why do you insist? Crews are easy to find. Even young pretty ones," she goaded.

"You are the only crew I need, my dear. Besides, we're ready to go. The provisions are replenished, the tanks are topped and the great adventure awaits us!"

"I suppose it could be fun to join the few boats that are heading out to the Galapagos. We could go that far with them, couldn't we? We'd have a little company at least part of the way and it wouldn't make the trip seem so lonely."

"You mean you don't want me all to yourself?" he grinned as he leered at her naked body.

"Do you ever think of anything other than what is in your pants?"

"Absolutely," he said, "I'm almost always thinking about what's in yours."

CHAPTER 5

Emerging from the locks, the *Mysteria* sailed into the Pacific Ocean only to be met with a wet and overcast sky. One day at the Balboa Yacht club was all that was allowed and so they set forth on the forty-five hundred mile leg to Hawaii. Lorenzo felt exhilarated. Karen was mortified. As the lights of Panama City flickered in the distance, Karen realized the enormous mistake she had made by agreeing to go. What if he struck first? Could she even go through with her own plan? She wasn't a murderess, yet her own survival depended on her strength of will. Within hours she was so deeply depressed that she could do little more than weep. Lorenzo, on the other hand, focused on the task before him. The captain had chosen a southern route hoping to avoid the hurricanes prevalent at that time of year in the North Pacific. He knew it was a little longer and far more desolate, a perfect setting for him to do what he needed to do. He also knew he had to keep the revised chart he had plotted away from Karen for the next few days, only allowing her access to the original one set for the Galapagos. After that it really wouldn't matter, they'd be well into the Pacific and there would be little, if anything, she could do. Karen was a strong woman, he reasoned. She'll pull out of this funk and be just fine. All she needed was a little good weather.

The arguments began just three days out of Panama. As the *Mysteria* made her way further and further south Karen anxiously awaited their arrival in the Galapagos. In spite of the overcast skies she would come topside and spend hours peering into the gray haze, hoping for some vestige of humanity to surface. As they approached the island of Malpelo, Karen and Lorenzo both felt an unease blanket their small boat. The inhospitable shoreline was notoriously cursed and said to have brought bad luck to those who dared sail near it. Lorenzo had calculated four to five hours to clear the rocky island, then he intended to tack, head due west into the open seas of the Pacific, and hold a steady course to Hawaii for the next fifty odd days. He only had to tolerate Karen for a few more weeks, he reasoned, then he'd have all the peace he wanted. He could sail the rest of the way to Hawaii in blissful solitude. Malpelo, though, seemed to have its own agenda.

Ten hours later the menacing island still remained on their port side. It was as if it had reached out and held the *Mysteria* in an inescapable grip. It frightened Karen, reminding her of the dreams where she envisioned the boat in pieces, strewn along the rocky shore.

"Malpelo is just plain evil," Karen whispered. "It's ugly, scarred, and besides, it reeks ... like the smell of death. Why on earth aren't we past it yet? You said a few hours at most. I don't like this, Lorenzo, it's as if the island wantsus ... and I think it wants us dead. Please, do something, and do it now ... I need to put this place behind us and see a few friendly faces."

"Believe me dear," he snapped, "I'm trying. It really is strange you know, there must be some kind of magnetic force in the water that holds us here. I'll start up the engine, motor a bit more West and see if we can't distance ourselves. I've often wondered what it is about this island that gives it such a bad reputation ... now I know. And you are right, the odor is nauseating," Lorenzo agreed. "What on earth could cause that? Not to worry, Karen, we'll pass it in a few hours and before you know it we'll be in Hilo."

"You mean the Galapagos, don't you? We *are* stopping aren't we? Lorenzo, you promised."

"There's no time mi amor, we're already late and we really need to keep on if we intend to beat the weather, you know that. We've been skirting south as it is, it's just too much of a risk. We'll have to head West shortly."

Karen was livid. She turned on Lorenzo with a rage. "You just can't stop lying, can you," she screamed. "You never intended to stop. You just thought telling me we could would keep me quiet. You really don't care if this trip is enjoyable for me at all. All you care about is you and your precious image as some kind of super sailor! Well let me tell you something mister, if you don't stop as you promised I'm going to make this trip a living hell for you. And you know damn well I can do it!"

"Yes, I know quite well you can do it. No, we're not going to stop. We're going to pass this damn island and keep right on going. We are into weather as it is, so *you* brace yourself for the storm outside and *I'll* brace myself for the storm inside and with any luck at all we'll both see Hawaii in one piece!"

"Lorenzo, I've been reading the chart, too. You have us going South all the way to Galapagos, did I miss something?"

"You didn't miss a thing, I just decided to plot a new course once we passed Malpelo, get us back on schedule and arrive in Hawaii safe and sound." Damn filthy rock, he thought, he hadn't counted on running into trouble this early or having to explain his change of direction quite so soon.

"Well, I can see that the charade is over," Karen sneered, "you're back to being yourself, the same selfish bastard you've always been. You haven't changed and you never will." Karen could have slapped him she was so angry, but instead she turned on her heel and went below. With every step she vowed to make him pay.

She clasped her hand tightly around the locket. She would put an end to the miserable marriage, an end to the two-timing, and an end to him. It would be a two month trek to Hawaii, but as she climbed into her bunk she wondered which one of them would ever see the islands.

CHAPTER 6

The ship's brass clock echoed eight bells as the *Mysteria* drove westward, sweeping easily over ten foot swells that surged out of the south. The billowy genoa pulled the boat forward while the staysail gently tugged, doing its small bit to keep the sloop on an even keel. They had come nearly 1200 miles from Panama and the deep blackness of the Pacific Ocean seemed more menacing than usual.

Thick, low clouds enveloped the *Mysteria* like an eerie shroud that neither moon nor star could penetrate. Only a solitary bright light burned steadily from the masthead like a beacon, proof to the world that here, in the midst of all darkness, life did indeed exist. A strong easterly current continued to slow their progress. Heavily loaded, the yacht was barely able to maintain a speed of three knots, putting them almost twenty-five miles a day behind schedule.

For nearly three weeks a cold and bitter war was fought on board. Lorenzo's arrogance and determination were overshadowed by his desire for serenity and before long even his beloved sea brought little comfort to him. He cursed Karen and wondered if being rid of her now might put things right again, certainly they were far enough out but it was as if something else lingered out there in the darkness, corrupting the harmony of the voyage. Being the practical man that he was, Lorenzo found it difficult to put faith in intuition. He had no use for omens and dreams. He believed in cause and effect. Yet lately this feeling of unease had taken root, burrowing itself deeper with each passing day. He blamed it on the weather. He blamed it on Malpelo. He blamed it on Karen. But in his heart, he knew it was none of those things ... it simply *was*.

It was after midnight when he finally turned away from the console. He had set the course and turned on the autopilot. As he descended the few steps that led from the cockpit he decided to take one last look around before refilling his coffee flask. Splashing sounds immediately caught his attention and peering into the darkness Lorenzo barely made out the sleek shapes that cut through the water. There appeared to be dozens of dolphins keeping pace with the boat, rising and falling softly like some kind of orchestrated lullaby. He could see Karen's familiar profile in the galley where she stood pouring a glass of wine. As much as he loathed her Lorenzo appreciated his wife's unusual affinity with nature and knew that she would enjoy the diversion of these delightful creatures. Whistling to her, he signaled her to come topside.

"Take a look out there, mi amor, it's a sensuous dance our friends are performing, and it's just for your pleasure. A gift, if you will."

Karen stiffened, hoping he hadn't seen her carefully open the locket and remove the small pill that nested within. She knew her time was short and she sensed that he would make his move soon. She had already calculated the distance they had sailed. Far enough out yet close enough for her to make the sail back alone. She would simply slip the lethal dose into his drink, offer it to him as a gesture of peace, let nature take its course and ... well, one less husband who has had an unfortunate accident at sea.

"Damn," she muttered with irritation, "timing is everything." Hastily she replaced the tablet into the hollow of the locket and made her way up to the cockpit. Karen peered over the railing and felt her anger lift like a veil.

"They're beautiful, Lorenzo! Look out there, I don't think I've ever seen so many."

Like a giddy child she raced down the companionway, reached the electrical panel, and switched on the spotlights. The small sailboat brilliantly glowed in the phosphorous light of the ocean. Karen could now clearly make out the dark figures and delighted in her new discovery.

"I'm afraid we are not being entertained by dolphins," Karen giggled. "These charming mammals, dear skipper, are whales, Pilot whales to be exact and there are literally hundreds of them!"

For hours the whales escorted the *Mysteria* across the Pacific. Karen had made her way below after being entertained by their attention, but Lorenzo remained at the helm keeping a watchful eye on the huge mammals. Once melodic, the mood however, had changed. Larger bull whales had replaced the younger calves and instead of their playful antics, the pod seemed increasingly agitated. They were so close to the hull Lorenzo could easily reach down and touch them. Within minutes the whales had sandwiched the boat. They were clearly angry now, their breathing erratic and their motions furious. The once soft whistling from their blow holes was now a piercing eruption of water. The Pilot whales were no longer friendly. Closing in, they tested the sides of the boat. The sloop groaned beneath the pressure. At first it was just a slight bump, then another, and suddenly a mighty jolt rocked the *Mysteria* as they pounded the sides of her hull. Horrified, Lorenzo steadied himself against the helm, then realized they intended to batter the small sailboat to pieces. He could see Karen being thrown from her bunk below like some kind of lifeless doll. When she raised her head he could see the terror in her eyes.

"My God," she screamed at him, "what's happening? The water's nearly up to my ankles! It's coming in fast, too fast. Lorenzo, we're sinking."

He couldn't believe it. He simply couldn't believe it. Momentarily stunned, Lorenzo shook himself to clear his head.

Racing below, he activated the bilge pump, but quickly realized the uselessness of it all. The sea water poured in as the tightened herd continued to crush the fiberglas hull. The water was now at his knees, Lorenzo lunged for the radio and began signaling a MAYDAY with their position. Instinctively, Karen grabbed a knife from the sink and climbed up to the deck. Reaching the dingy, she cut away the plastic bag that held the life raft. Dragging it to the cockpit she could hear Lorenzo's steady pleas over the radio. Only minutes had passed but the boat was going down quickly. It was time now; time to inflate the raft, load what they could and abandon the *Mysteria*.

Together they gathered the few things they could reach and loaded the small life raft. A comforter served as a sack to fill with as many tins of food as Karen's arms could carry, a first aid kit, flare gun and a flashlight. Lorenzo tossed in the water purifier, log book and a few spiral notebooks. As the water reached the deck they hastily tried to slide the oval raft over the stern. Catching on something it dangled for a moment in mid air, but putting a little muscle into it they managed to lower it into the sea. Karen slid quickly onto the safety of the raft and turned to see Lorenzo securing the bow line to the *Mysteria*.

"Are you crazy?" She shouted. "What the hell are you doing?"

"There are still a few things I can get," he yelled back. "Things we need. Besides, I can't leave her yet. She's my whole life Karen, I just can't leave her yet."

"Make it quick skipper, I am not going to be pulled down by a sinking ship just because you want to say goodbye." The few minutes she watched her husband seemed like an eternity to Karen, and then she screamed again, "Get in now Lorenzo, or I swear I'll cut the line myself!"

"Okay," he said grudgingly, "I'm coming." As he pulled in the twenty foot line the heavy swells tossed the small lifeboat, knocking it against the stern of the sloop. Suddenly a gush of air escaped from the raft. Karen looked down in horror as one end deflated beneath her. Even before she could react, there was a small popping sound as a rush of air filled the backup chamber. In no time the raft was once again solid and bobbing against the stern of the *Mysteria*. Carefully, Lorenzo handed Karen the last few things he had managed to salvage for survival, then lifted his heavy frame onto the overloaded raft and shoved hard off the stern, distancing themselves from the doomed sailboat. He was weeping openly now, unashamed at the tide of emotion that swept over him for this long and loyal friend. Lorenzo had sailed her for over twenty-three years and now after only twenty minutes he watched helplessly as she sank to her death. The whales had mysteriously vanished, the sea was no longer a bubbling cauldron of black fins. Karen and Lorenzo held each other tightly and watched silently as the last bit of the *Mysteria* slipped beneath the water.

PART 2

THE RAFT

CHAPTER 1

◄○►

In the last hour before dawn there wasn't a star to be seen nor even a sliver of moon to betray the darkness, a darkness that wrapped itself around the small raft like a tight fitting glove. A slight drizzle fell while the sea rocked the six foot rubber lifeboat as if it were cradled in God's arms. Still in shock, Lorenzo and Karen lay side by side silently weeping, each reliving the last horrendous hour.

Lorenzo struggled to bring his mind back to the present. The *Mysteria* gone, the Pilot whales gone, and now only an ill equipped raft was all that kept them from certain death. He knew he had to reassure her, say something to convince her that all would be well, even if it meant lying. He was a good liar, he knew. He had done it so many times before without her suspecting. But this wasn't like the casual dalliances he had successfully shielded from Karen. He knew full well that if his MAYDAY had not been received then their chances of survival would be slim. This time he prayed she wouldn't question him, that she would just accept his lie. Groping for the right words Lorenzo gently took Karen's hand and brought it to his lips.

"Sleep, mi amor, sleep. They'll find us soon. I promise." Unable to say anything further, he closed his eyes, curled his large frame around Karen and allowed his exhausted body a few moments rest.

As the hours passed the soft rain stopped and eventually a small ray of sunshine drifted in and out of the clouded skies. It was late afternoon of the first day when they looked out onto the vast ocean that surrounded them. Composing himself, Lorenzo slowly shook his head in disbelief.

"Who would ever have thought? Who would ever believe? My God, we were sunk by a bunch of damn whales. The *Mysteria* gone ... and in only twenty minutes. Jesus, Karen, I don't understand it."

"I've never heard of whales behaving like that," Karen stammered. "It's right out of *Moby Dick*, only this wasn't some fictitious tale, it actually happened. You wouldn't listen to me when I told you I knew something dreadful was going to happen, that my dreams really do mean something, that my premonitions aren't just fantasy. Now look where we are!" Her mind still reeling she added, "And if that MAYDAY wasn't picked up they'll never find us, we're going to die here, aren't we?"

"No, Karen, we're not." He could almost smell her fear and his state of mind wasn't any better. For the first time in his life he was actually scared. He didn't want to die like this anymore than she did.

"We are going to survive ... whatever it takes, we're going to survive," he promised.

"And you had to tear a hole in the damn raft forcing it over the stern! All in all, I guess that's my good fortune," Karen snapped.

"What the Hell is that supposed to mean? I'm going to have to try to patch it or we'll be pumping air into that chamber till we're lucky enough to be picked up."

"My point exactly. We. Don't think for one minute I didn't know what you were planning. Middle of the damn ocean ... accidents happen, don't they? Rough seas, wife overboard, not a single soul to dispute it. Perfect plan, until now that is. Now you need me. To save yourself, you have to save me. That silly little patch is like a Band-Aid on a gaping wound. No way is that going to hold. We are going to have to pump. You and I, my dear, pump till hell freezes over!"

"Are you delirious or just exhausted? Undoubtedly both. I swear, sometimes I just have to wonder what goes through your mind. Kill you? Admittedly, there have been times when I could ring your neck, but actually murder you? Ridiculous."

She was right and he knew it. She had that damn sixth sense about her, almost like reading your mind. Never mind he thought, I need her help now and it will be far easier to convince her that she has an over active imagination.

"You'd be better off focusing on the problem we have at hand, and that is surviving till we are rescued."

"Rescued? Now who's delirious? We're in the middle of the ocean in a raft that won't even hold air. Even if the radio signal did get through, which I seriously doubt, it would be like finding a needle in a haystack. Our chances of being found are slim to none. Our only hope is God. I've been praying ever since I first stepped into this raft, Lorenzo, praying like never before that God would deliver us from this nightmare. I even bargained. Yes, my dear, I made a deal with God."

"And that would be?" Lorenzo was strangely curious.

"If you must know, I took a vow of celibacy if He would see us safely home," she said stiffly.

"Now I know you're nuts," he laughed. "You think God will save us if you give up sex? Why not just throw me overboard right now! Better yet, I'll just jump!"

"Go ahead, better you than me. You can make your little jokes, but if we're saved we will see who has the last laugh." Angrily Karen swaddled herself in the damp comforter, she shivered as she turned her back to Lorenzo and pressed herself against one side of the small raft.

The whole conversation had seemed strangely erotic to Lorenzo. He felt himself growing aroused and wanted her more than ever.

"Well, God helps those who help themselves," he quipped, "and with your cooperation I intend to help myself right now."

Squeezing ever closer, he threw his arm over Karen's waist and yanked her body next to his.

"Are you deaf," she railed in disgust, "first you plan to kill me and now you want to have your way with me? I made a vow mister, a vow I intend to keep, so back off and leave me alone."

"How dare you," he lashed out, "how dare you make a promise that directly involves me."

"Easy. I want to see dry land again and if giving up sex with a cheating, treacherous, over sexed latin is part of the deal, well count me in."

"You're a cruel woman, Karen, but this conversation is far from over. I'll just have to revisit it when you're thinking a little clearer."

Rolling over, Lorenzo's passion had all but disappeared. He needed sleep, there'd be plenty of time to assess the damaged raft, their position, and how long they could last until they were picked up. It never once occurred to him that the two months it would take to sail to Hawaii on the *Mysteria* would be spent drifting in open water on a weekend raft.

CHAPTER 2

The few hours sleep was welcomed and by the next morning Lorenzo had put his anger to rest. He gently nudged Karen, hoping she had done the same. Still drowsy, she braced against one end of the raft and pulled herself up.

"I'm sorry Lorenzo, I'm just frightened to death and I don't see any way out of this. I suppose we're doomed," she said hoping for some reassurance.

"Not just yet Karen, but it is time to take stock of what we managed to salvage and check out that leak," he said confidently. "I feel sure we'll be picked up within a week, ten days at most. Even if they didn't get the signal when the kids don't hear from us they'll be all over the Coast Guard."

"I pray to God you're right, but you won't mind if I send a few mental messages, will you? I know you think they're foolish but they certainly can't hurt."

"Can't hurt." he echoed. "See if you can't find a pen and some paper at your end, there's nothing like that over here."

"I know I grabbed some, ah, here they are." Reaching under the pile of provisions Karen lifted a pad and pen from the debris. "I'm ready."

"Let's see, the raft's already equipped with paddles, pump, patches, flashlights, knife, whistle and flares. Karen, I'll call off what's at my end, then you do the same. OK? Compass, desalinator, gloves," he began. Lorenzo continued until he ran out of items at his end then took the pad and pen from Karen and jotted down all that she had bunched around her. A few clothes, her toiletry case, some blankets and a pitiful amount of food. She had managed to throw in a small radio, a deck of cards and as luck would have it, a six-pack of beer.

"We're in great shape, my dear," he smiled. "We'll just ration what we've got, fish, and pretend we're on vacation! Hell, we've got a rod and reel. Not a thing wrong with sushi, is there?"

"Very funny. I guess you are right, it could be a lot worse. But what about the tear? Is it patchable?"

"Well, it's a very slow leak, shouldn't be a problem. I'll see if I can take care of it now while there's light."

With patch in hand Lorenzo then slid over the edge and located the rip. Within twenty minutes he was back on board.

"Mission accomplished," he said proudly. "Hand me the pump and let's blow her back up."

Karen pushed the pump over to him and watched nervously as he slid one end of the bellows into the valve. Securing it, he pumped for a few minutes until the small raft felt firm once again beneath them. The relief showed on his face as he turned to Karen,

"We're back in business," he grinned.

Before the sun set they managed to erect the canopy already provided in the raft, arrange the provisions and carve a niche for themselves that although tight, seemed acceptable.

"Well, at least we'll be dry for a while. I know it's not the Ritz, but it's a roof over our heads," Lorenzo said earnestly.

"Some roof," Karen laughed. "We do have windows though, and that's a consolation. I could peek out and see the stars if there were any, but it looks pretty grim out there."

"At least you're laughing about it. We've got to keep a positive attitude and pull together on this Karen or we'll never make it."

"You're right, Lorenzo, let's call a truce. I promise to be good if you promise to get us out of this mess. Fair?"

"Not exactly," he chuckled, "but I'll take what I can get. OK, truce. Let's shake on it." As he reached across to take her hand Karen reared back.

"I don't think so mister, you're ogling! Give you a hand and you'll be all over me! We're dry, somewhat comfortable and I know exactly what's going through your head, so just forget it. I'm all for the truce, but there will be no shaking, bumping, or even the least bit of grinding. Got it?"

"You said you'd be good. I just thought you meant *very* good. Fine. Consider yourself left alone. For now. I'm not going to give up, though, you should know that."

"I know it, so stop pouting and figure out what the evening ration is going to be, and by that I mean food."

"Hmm, I don't think it would hurt to have a cheese cracker, a few raisins, and how about if we split a beer?"

"Sounds perfect." Karen couldn't understand why she was in such high spirits, maybe she was still in shock. Maybe she was delirious. Maybe she had just come to terms with it all. But whatever the reason, she was smiling.

CHAPTER 3

◄○►

The very first evening on the raft the sky had been starless. In the days that followed what had started out as a gentle rain soon turned threatening and as the seas swelled the storm battered the small craft. The canopy held tight, a little water seeped through the window flaps, they bailed as best they could and rode it out. The weather continued to be miserable for the next week. Gray, rainy, and rough. The slow leak persisted and they found themselves having to pump nearly every hour. Karen's mood, too, had taken a turn for the worse. Exhausted and depressed she railed against Lorenzo. She blamed him for everything, for getting sunk, for not stopping in the Galapagos, for being an egotistical prick. Pointing her finger at him she accused,

"You just had to be rid of me, didn't you? Couldn't just get a divorce like a normal person, no, you had to get me out in the middle of the ocean and erase me completely. Afraid you'd have to pay alimony?"

"That's enough, Karen," Lorenzo hissed. "You're being ridiculous and I can't listen to it another minute. I thought we had a truce. I'm doing everything I can to keep us both alive right now so humor me and shut up."

Karen lowered her head and began to cry. "Sorry. I'm so sorry. I don't want to die in the middle of the Pacific, Lorenzo, not like this. Promise me we'll make it, promise me we'll be rescued," she pleaded.

"I promise," he sighed. Grateful that her tirade had ended he turned to the valve. "You ready to give me a hand with this pump now?"

The next morning the sun shone brightly. A cool breeze stirred as the raft drifted aimlessly on a calm ocean. Taking advantage of the good weather, they raised the flaps from the windows and let the fresh air dry the inside of the lifeboat. Relaxing for the first time, Karen leaned on the edge of the raft and peered into the emptiness. Scanning the sea she bolted upright. A small, triangular head had broken the surface and was making its way toward them.

"Lorenzo, quick, is that what I think it is?"

Sliding next to her he grinned.

"If you're thinking turtle, you're right. It's probably looking for shade and figures we'll do nicely. It's not that big either, I think I can grab it as it goes under the raft between the chambers. We might just have a proper dinner tonight." Composing himself so as not frighten the poor thing, he slipped on the sailing gloves and waited until it was directly below them making its way toward the small air pocket beneath the lifeboat. Deftly, he reached down and grabbed the shell, plucking it from its path. In one smooth movement he raised the turtle upward and swung it through the window, dropping it on the comforter Karen had arranged next to him. Knife in hand, Karen quickly separated its head from its body.

"Well done, my dear, if not a bit grisly," he beamed.

"Thank you, captain, and kudos to you as well. You were absolutely magnificent! Just think, Lorenzo, turtle soup, turtle filet, and leg of turtle, it's a veritable feast!"

"And let's not forget about turtle bait," he added. "This little baby will get us a ton of fish. Hand me the desalinator Karen, and let's make some fresh water for our *soup de jour*."

The anticipation of meat had done wonders for them both. Laughing and joking with each other, they readied their meal, then gorged themselves without the thought of rationing a single morsel.

For the first time in a very long time they were getting along as well as they had when they first met.

"Do you recall," she began, "our first date? I remember you were so dashing, so very handsome, and you took me to that charming little bistro just off the beach. You stared at me all night."

"Oh, I was smitten, all right," he laughed, "you were the loveliest creature I had ever laid eyes on. I remember having to choose my words so carefully so as not to frighten you off. It was the most wonderful evening, and I'm sure that was the very moment I fell in love with you."

Dreamily, they brought themselves back to reality. They capped the day off with a few hands of gin rummy and watched as the sun slipped beneath the horizon. They had been taking turns with the bellows, as one rested the other pumped air into the small raft all the while keeping an eye out for any signs of rescue. Taking the first shift of the evening, Lorenzo watched Karen doze. Neither one could actually sleep, they were both still so traumatized. The meal had done wonders for her, though, and for a brief moment she seemed at peace. It had been over two weeks, Lorenzo was quite sure now that help would not be coming. Tears rolled down his cheeks as the realization of their situation sunk in. They probably were not going to make it.

The wind had picked up that evening and as the raft rode the crests, the ballast did its job keeping them upright. Suddenly Karen was brought up to attention by first one bump, then another. Bump, bump, bump. Karen's eyes mirrored her terror. Lorenzo put his finger to his lips signaling her to keep quiet, not to say a word.

"Sharks," he whispered. "I'm surprised they've stayed away this long. They're testing the raft."

"God," she nearly screamed.

"Hush, Karen, be very quiet and very, very still," he warned. He hoped the sharks would abandon their inspection if no movement were detected. All it would take is one good bite to the raft and they would be doomed. It was a terrifying thirty minutes before he was sure they had gone.

"I'm afraid we haven't seen the last of them. They'll be back. They'll follow us for awhile, continue to bump and eventually, if we manage to stay afloat, they'll leave."

"They're eating machines, Lorenzo," she wailed. "They don't think, they just eat, and we're on the menu. The thought of dying that way, oh God Lorenzo, I'd rather shoot myself."

"I know you're scared. So am I. But we have to keep our heads and be still while they check us out. Have faith. I promised you we would make it through, didn't I? Remember?" He knew she was petrified. He reached out and put his arms around her. Hugging her, he said quietly, "Trust me, we're going to make it."

CHAPTER 4

Nearly thirty days on the raft and not a ship had passed. The rain continued to beat down upon them, the sharks relentlessly battered them, and yet they stayed afloat. The patch, though, had given way and they were now forced to pump every half-hour. They prayed for a break in the weather. Lorenzo could only hope that the lack of radio contact would cause his sons enough concern to alert the Coast Guard. A slim chance at best that they would be found, but it was all he had to hold onto. He had managed to catch a few fish and Karen had continued to ration the meager amount of food they had salvaged from the *Mysteria*, but they were both losing weight at an alarming pace and the confining quarters had cramped their once large frames. Water that had puddled on the floor of the raft had ultimately created oozing, foul smelling sores across their bodies.

Like a ritual, Karen would take a bit of the aloe cream she had found in the First Aid Kit and gently massage her husband's aching limbs, then he would do the same for her. It was a small gesture that helped more mentally than physically, bringing them closer together. Every now and then she would touch his cheek and smile, understanding that even in the face of death he hid his fear from her. His respect for her grew as well as she fiercely clung to hope, refusing to give up.

They filled the following days with gin rummy games and fantasized about the great feast they would have once they were rescued. Karen did her best to keep her depression from showing and honor the truce they had agreed upon.

"Sounds like the rain is finally letting up, Lorenzo. What do you think? Why not pop your head out there and check it out?"

"Good idea. If I can see the stars I might be able to get a heading."

Twisting his large frame Lorenzo lifted the flap and stared up at the sky. The rain had stopped and miraculously the clouds had disappeared.

"Thank God," he whispered. "Looks like we're on a steady course east, we should hit the coast before too long. At least the wind is giving us a good push that way. First light I'm going to do something about that patch. Give ourselves a breather and maybe a few hours of continuous rest."

"Sounds like a plan," Karen agreed.

Eagerly they awaited the dawn and when the stars faded and the sun came up they looked at each other with relief. Lorenzo grabbed another patch and set to mending the tear immediately. Karen did her best to spread the comforter on the canopy to dry. She sopped up the water that gathered on the floor of the raft and arranged the remaining provisions as if she were decorating a new home. Satisfied that it looked presentable, she laughed.

"It's almost cozy, don't you think?"

"Not exactly *Architectural Digest* material but certainly *Better Homes and Gardens*," he joked. "Really, Karen, it's great. You're quite the little home maker." They had been getting along famously lately, both realizing that they needed each other to overcome the ordeal they faced.

"Now how about if I do my part and put some food on the table, it's a beautiful day for fishing."

Wincing in pain, he picked up the rod and reel, baited the hook and cast the line. Within minutes he had a hit.

"It's a big one honey," he yelled excitedly. "Gotta be over fifty pounds!"

Lorenzo struggled to bring the fish in but for every two feet he reeled in, the creature would regain four. It was a battle of wills and although exhausted, Lorenzo finally started to make some headway. He nearly had it to the raft when a sudden jerk from the great fish snapped the rod and the line went limp.

"Crap," he screamed in frustration. Collapsing at one end of the raft Lorenzo gasped, "I had him, Karen, I know I had him. Felt like a damn whale. Lost the pole, the bait and the hook. The *only* hook. We've still got line, though, we need something small and shiny. Give me your locket," he demanded.

"Are you nuts?" Clutching the heirloom she dared not let him find the lethal pill that still nested inside. "Do you know how long this locket has been in my family?" Karen cried. "You think I'm going to hand it over to you to feed some stupid fish? No way. Never. If I have to die of starvation with this around my neck, so be it. Find something else."

She quickly turned her back to him hoping he wouldn't notice her shaking hands. They hadn't argued in weeks and she hadn't thought of the pill since the night of the sinking. Karen knew she couldn't explain the tablet, and she wasn't about to toss it. It still could be useful. She'd take it herself before she'd let the sharks have her, and if they managed to survive ... well, that was something else to think about.

Lorenzo was stunned by her overreaction. He knew the locket was meaningful to her, but this? He thought Karen would appreciate the fact that their survival was damn more important. But he was in no mood to argue with her now. He was hungry, tired, and determined to catch a fish, even if meant with his own blistered hands. He had seen trigger fish come to the surface whenever they discarded anything over the side. Putting the gloves back on,

Lorenzo crushed a cheese cracker up and sprinkled it over the water next to the window. True to form the trigger fish raced to the surface, then a small grouper. Plunging his hands in the water Lorenzo grabbed the grouper first, successfully flipping it into the raft. Then as quickly he hauled in a few triggers. It wasn't nearly as hard as he thought it would be. Filleting the fish, Lorenzo placed a few strips of meat in front of Karen.

"Didn't need your damn locket anyhow. Eat up."

CHAPTER 5

The sun held for the next four days and they reveled in its warmth. Lorenzo was able to catch a few more fish, they replenished their water supply, and played cards. The sharks were a constant threat, though, bumping, testing, never giving them a moment's peace. A fifteen foot hammerhead plagued them for two days. Aggressive and menacing, he'd spin the lifeboat around like a top, scaring them to death. Finally, he gave up, never to be seen again. As much as they loved the sun, it brought its own set of problems. Turtles. Turtles with barnacles. They loved the shade the raft provided and would surface between the air chambers, scraping their backs against the floor of the rubber lifeboat. Karen would grab an oar, prod them out from under, then give them a mighty whack until they would swim leisurely away. At one point two of the turtles created such a ruckus that Karen was nearly hysterical. She couldn't push them out and she was sure that they would rip the raft to shreds.

"Do something, Lorenzo," she yelled.

"Feels like somebody's getting real lucky down there, if you know what I mean," he snickered. "See, birds do it, turtles do it, why in the hell can't we do it? I realize we're weak but I can't imagine a better way to spend the afternoon."

"Because we can't. Now just let it go and get rid of those damn turtles before we become fish food. Will you *please*?"

"Fine, but I expect to be well rewarded for my efforts." Taking the oar from Karen, Lorenzo shoved it under the raft and rammed the two love makers. Three more jabs and they got the message.

"Happy now?"

"Yes, and you should be too. What if they had torn a hole that you couldn't patch? Huh? What then?"

He knew it was possible, and she was probably right. In an effort to calm her Lorenzo spoke gently, "I'll keep a better watch on them, I promise. Now, about that reward. It's been a long time, please, just a little cuddle time? Call it therapeutic."

"I'm not calling it anything at all. Have you forgotten my vow? There will be no sex aboard this raft, unless of course, you want to take care of your problem single handedly."

"I just might do that, missy," he shot back. "It'll be your loss."

"I'll get over it," she said dryly.

She knew he was angry. He had turned his back to her, flattening himself against one side of the raft. Hoping to distract him, she picked up the pump, secured it into the valve and began the ritual of replenishing air into the chambers. After a few moments Lorenzo rolled over and placed his hand on the bellows.

"Here, let me do that."

They had endured six tormenting weeks on the raft, surviving squalls, endless rain and the never-ending battering by tenacious sharks. Turtles continued to be a problem and a tear in the canopy had left them soaked and miserable. The sores on their bodies had only gotten worse and the cramped quarters had stiffened their joints. The weather had taken its toll on not only Lorenzo and Karen, but the raft as well. They were now pumping air every twenty minutes. The lack of sleep showed on their haggard faces.

It was just after dawn when they heard the low hum of a passing freighter. Pushing the window flaps aside Lorenzo stared in horror at the ship bearing down on them. Barely two hundred yards away, it was moving fast and would surely run them down if they didn't do something quickly to distance themselves from its path.

"Give me the oar Karen, you get the flare," he shouted. Using his last bit of strength he expertly guided the lifeboat away from the approaching bow while Karen searched frantically for the gun.

"I can't load it, my God, it won't open, it's stuck," she panicked. The freighter was now alongside them and not showing any signs of slowing. "The flashlight, grab the flashlight," she wailed.

Reaching behind him Lorenzo retrieved the torch and held it out the window. Tapping the flashlight he gave the universal SOS code over and over. He scanned the deck and pilot house for any sign of life as the ship passed rapidly by them. Their waving and shouting for help had gone unseen and unheard. As the freighter became nothing more than a speck in the distance they both wept. "Why, Lorenzo, just tell me why, haven't we suffered enough? Aren't our lives worth anything? Why didn't they stop?"

"I don't know, I don't have all the answers for you, but I do know we don't need that damn ship. We're going to make it on our own. No matter how far, no matter how long. We are going to survive this. I swear."

As the tears of frustration fell down his cheeks Lorenzo held Karen, finding comfort in her closeness. Stroking her hair softly, he realized the failed rescue had only steeled his determination to prevail. Lorenzo's emotions had come full circle. He had loved her, hated her, depended on her and now, what? Was he feeling love for her all over again? Without a doubt the small raft had brought a reconciliation between them. Was this really God's way of telling him that their marriage was meant to last? Was it his destiny to end up here in the middle of the ocean and change his ways? The only thing he knew for sure was that his feelings for Karen had changed.

CHAPTER 6

In the days that followed the weather broke, creating balmy days and warm, starlit nights. The current had kept them on a steady easterly course. Although painfully slow, Lorenzo now felt sure they would eventually drift back to the coast. They had already spotted one small island on the horizon. Too far off to row to but Lorenzo hoped the breeze would blow them close enough to reach it. After several hours it became obvious that they were drifting far north of the island and would see it disappear in short order.

The food supply from the *Mysteria* had been depleted and they were now solely dependent on what they could catch. A small turtle was a luxury, dorado when they were lucky, and trigger fish just to sustain themselves. Tirelessly, they patched, sewed, and taped the *Bob-Along Cassidy,* as they had christened the raft, pumping air into the chambers every thirty or forty minutes without fail. The sharks, still a constant threat, were noticeably thinning out, a sure sign that they were nearing the coast. The deck of cards had been lost to the water, forcing them to create diversions of their own. Charades, hang man, tic-tac-toe, but most enjoyed was a game of their own creation ... *make up a menu.* Fabulous meals were designed in their heads and as they supped on their meager trigger fish they imagined they were dining on a succulent leg of lamb or filet mignon.

Eight weeks had now passed and as dark clouds gathered they braced themselves for yet another bout of poring rain and stormy seas. Lorenzo wondered how much more the lifeboat could take. He was amazed that it had lasted this long. Just a little longer, he prayed, just get us to the coast. He thought he could already see the faint outline that defined a mountainous land mass and hoped it wasn't just his eyes playing tricks on him or a mirage that often accompanies isolation and fear.

"Let's make some fresh water before this storm hits. We can't afford to get dehydrated now and start hallucinating. I know I see land and if the wind blows hard enough it'll push us right to the beach. It's that close."

"I saw it, too," so weak she could barely speak. "I didn't want to say anything for fear I was losing my mind, but if you see it then it can't be a mirage, it must be real, right?"

"It's real, mi amor, by God, it's real. Pray for wind and lots of it."

It rained steadily for the next five days, the wind blew hard propelling the *Bob-Along* closer and closer to land. Lorenzo and Karen would take turns straining their eyes through the pouring rain to catch a glimpse of the coastline. Nearer and nearer, the closer it appeared the more hopeful they became. They could hear passing ships but with visibility so bad, they doubted they would be seen. They just prayed they wouldn't be hit or sucked under a massive rudder.

The dawn of the sixth day the sun came up bright and clear. They struggled to lower the canopy, and gazed at the beautiful sight just miles away. Weak and near death, they could hardly believe their eyes. After more than two long months they had finally made it. Clutching each other Lorenzo finally spoke.

"I told you we'd make it, mi amor, didn't I? And now I'm going to make you another promise. Things are going to be different from here on out. I do love you and you have shown your love for me. I'll always keep you safe, you can count on it."

"I know," Karen whispered, "I suppose it just took an act of God for us both to realize that the love was still there. We got through this with His help."

Holding him tightly, she allowed him to gently kiss her lips. Tenderly he laid her down across the floor of the raft, placed his arm beneath her head and made love to her. It was if they had never left that small cafe where they had first fallen in love. Their bodies nested together, they fell into a deep sleep, their first in a very long time.

PART 3

THE RESCUE

CHAPTER 1

It seemed they had slept for hours. When they awoke Karen and Lorenzo held each other and wept. Their unbelievable journey had come to an end. Gazing at the stretch of land before them, Lorenzo spoke.

"We're too weak to row and it's too far to swim. Besides, our bodies would give out long before we ever reached the beach. The tide will bring us in, just rest now, Karen, we're almost home."

"But we're so close," she cried, "so very close. What if the current pushes us away? What if we end up back at sea? I don't think I can last another day."

"Trust me, you won't have to. We're drifting toward the shore. I'm not sure where we are, but I suspect its somewhere off the coast of South America. We might even be picked up by a fishing boat if we're lucky. Go back to sleep, dream about a warm bath and hot food," he coaxed.

"You'll be all right pumping alone?"

"I'm good for now. I'll wake you if I need you."

Closing her eyes Karen felt her body relax for the first time in two long months. The sharks had ceased their endless battering and had seemed to vanish. The turtles, too, had given up their constant scratching. It was quiet, and the gentle rocking of the raft lulled her into yet another restful sleep. She dreamed of her children, her mother, and the *Mysteria*. She dreamed of Lorenzo. She dreamed of home.

It was late afternoon when Lorenzo woke her.

"Karen sit up, look," he said hoarsely. "There's a boat headed right for us and it's slowing down. They've spotted us. They're going to pick us up, looks like a fishing boat."

"Yell, Lorenzo, wave something, let them know we're alive and need help!"

As the small trawler pulled up alongside them the crew gathered at the railing and stared down in horror. The raft was in shreds, the two passengers looked half dead, and the stench was dreadful. Two men quickly lowered a ladder and tossed a line to Lorenzo who held it tightly while they brought the *Bob-Along Cassidy* to their port side. Nuzzled against the hull, Karen was the first to reach them. Unable to stand she perched on her knees and raised her arms. Clasping her wrists, they lifted her up and onto the boat with ease. She was light as air, a mere skeleton. Lorenzo followed, his hands unsteady yet gripping the ladder with all his remaining strength. The two sailors caught hold of him and raised him to the deck.

"Thank God, thank you," was all he could say before passing out.

The captain of the boat that had rescued them had quickly radioed to shore, requesting an ambulance meet them at the dock. Karen and Lorenzo had been lifted onto stretchers and transported to the nearest hospital where they were received with all the flurry of arriving celebrities. Surrounded by nurses, Karen clung to the gold locket around her neck, refusing to allow them to remove it as they gently undressed her and tended to her oozing sores. Lorenzo lay helpless as the doctors examined him from head to toe, inserted an IV drip and dressed his badly wounded body.

They spent three weeks in the hospital, assailed by the press who clamored for every detail of their ordeal. The family had been flown in the next day and reunited with parents whom they believed to have perished at sea. Weak and emaciated, Lorenzo and Karen gathered their children around them and spoke of the traumatic journey.

"We survived by sheer will," Lorenzo recalled proudly. "I promised your mother we'd make it and we did. We made it ... together."

"Yes," Karen agreed, "we were a real team. We wouldn't have survived otherwise. Things are going to be different now. We have lived through the worst and we both understand the meaning of loyalty." They had both buried the anger and frustration that had once lingered under the surface. They had mended their broken marriage and the renewal of affection was obvious. They had only to heal their their wounds and begin life again.

CHAPTER 2

T he months following their release from the hospital were blissful, it was as if they had just met and had fallen in love all over again. Lorenzo had been attentive and doting, Karen the perfect wife. It was nearing the one year anniversary of their rescue when sshe began to suspect her husband had returned to his old ways. Late nights, lame excuses and the slightest trace of perfume on his clothes brought back old memories from a lifetime ago.

At first, she broached him carefully, not wanting to accuse him outright. But as the weeks passed, it became so blatant that Karen could not contain herself. She soon became the nagging wife she had left behind so very long ago. And then the dreams started up again. She wasn't on a boat, nor a raft, instead she was in her own home, lying on the tile gasping for breath. She could see Lorenzo standing over her body sneering at her, not lifting a finger to help her. He was going to try to kill her after all, she knew it.

Karen was so angry with herself that she had been taken in by him again. She cursed herself for abandoning her pledge to God and giving her body to Lorenzo before they had even been saved. In a rage, she opened the locket and stared at the small pill still resting in its hollow, thankful that she had never discarded it. You won't get away with it you bastard, she promised herself silently, I had a plan too and maybe now is the time to see it through.

Lorenzo and Karen readied themselves for the intimate dinner they had talked about to celebrate the one year anniversary of their incredible survival. Smartly dressed, Lorenzo nervously paced the living room floor while Karen busied herself in the kitchen. He had given a lot of thought to his feelings regarding his wife. He had loved her, of that he was sure, and he had tried for a while to be the man she wanted, but he knew in his heart that he would never be the husband she so desperately needed and she began to take every opportunity to blame him for their terrifying ordeal. He had come to the conclusion that he couldn't live with it any longer.

Looking up an old sailing buddy, Lorenzo managed to get the very thing he needed. The veteran seaman had his sources and although scarce, he produced a small vial of Blue-Ringed Octopus venom. Ten times more deadly than a cobra, the venom kills within minutes. Untraceable, there's no known antidote and he had warned Lorenzo to be very careful with it. To Lorenzo's relief, the old man asked no questions.

Karen had already set the table, paying careful attention to every detail. It had to be perfect, she thought to herself. Pulling two champagne flutes from the shelf, she then reached for the *Dom Perignon* and slowly poured a generous amount in each. Karen wrapped her hands tightly around the old gold locket, then let her fingers nimbly pop it open. Retrieving the small white pill, she quickly dropped it in the glass and watched as it dissolved.

"No better time than now," she smiled. "I promised myself you'd not get away with it; that you'd pay for not only years of heartache but the nightmare of a voyage that nearly killed us both. Now, my dear, you will."

She pushed through the french doors that led to the dining room, placed the glasses at the head of each place setting, and lit the candles.

"Champagne's on," she called to him.

"I'll be right there mi amor," he said. Fumbling in his pocket, Lorenzo clasped the thin vial of Blue-Ringed Octopus venom and proceeded to dinner. Everything looked marvelous; she had outdone herself. Too bad, he thought, but then at least she'll go out on an impressive note.

"Everything looks spectacular, but where are the flowers I brought for the table?"

"Oh my God, you're right! Give me a moment, will you, they're just in the kitchen."

As she rushed by, Lorenzo quickly slipped the vial from his trousers and poured the lethal venom into her glass. Within minutes she glided by him, setting the bouquet down.

"Ready?"

"Absolutely." He stood and handed Karen her glass.

Raising them together Lorenzo boldly toasted, "Here's to our second chance mi amor."

"Yes," Karen echoed, "a tiny sneer tugging at the corner of her mouth, "our second chance." As they savored the champagne their eyes locked for what seemed a lifetime but was only the briefest of moments, then the silence was broken by the sound of a single glass shattering on the tile. As the body slumped to the floor, the remaining flute was carefully placed on the dining table. Footsteps could be heard padding across the room to the wall telephone, the receiver was lifted from the cradle, the number dialed.

"911, What is your emergency? Yes, I've got your address and I'm sending an ambulance, it should be there in just a few minutes," the operator answered. "Would you like to stay on the line till they arrive?"

"It's not necessary, I've been through worse than this," was all the young lady heard then the line went dead.

EPILOGUE

As I held the latest invitation in my hand I recalled the utter amazement I had felt when reading about the miraculous rescue of Lorenzo and Karen Orozco. Everyone had thought them dead, lost at sea, and yet they had drifted for over two months and a thousand miles before they were picked up by a fishing boat off Ecuador. They had survived. Underweight and undernourished, both had been hospitalized for a time and released. Then news of the shocking death. I attended the funeral, offered my condolences, and thought what a cruel twist of fate life could take. I read the papers and followed the talk show appearances with interest until, like everything else, it became old news. Still, the card intrigued me. A Bon Voyage party for the *Mysteria II*. Crazy, I thought, just plain crazy, but this time I think I'll go.

ABOUT THE AUTHOR

A veteran sailor himself, Jason Simmons has long been a member of boating communities throughout the world. Raised in the Orient and educated in Europe, he currently resides in Prescott, Arizona.